My Mongolia

Illustrated by
Art Teacher, Erdenechuulun, and the
5th Grade Art Class in Nalaikh, Mongolia

Karen Gustafson

Beaver's Pond Press, Inc.
Edina, Minnesota

Copyright © 2004 by Karen Gustafson

All rights reserved. No part of this book may be reproduced in any form whatsoever, by photography or xerography or by any other means, by broadcast or transmission, by translation into any kind of language, nor by recording electronically or otherwise, without permission in writing from the publisher, except by a reviewer, who may quote brief passages in critical articles or reviews.

ISBN 1-59298-068-6

Library of Congress Catalog Number: 2004105631

Book design and typesetting: Mori Studio
Cover design: Mori Studio

Printed in the United States of America

First Printing: May 2004

07 06 05 04   6 5 4 3 2 1

Beaver's Pond Press, Inc.

7104 Ohms Lane, Suite 216
Edina, MN 55439
(952) 829-8818
www.BeaversPondPress.com

to order, visit *www.BookHouseFulfillment.com* or call 1-800-901-3480. Reseller discounts available.

Pronunciation Guide

Double vowels indicate a syllable is accented and that the vowel sound is held a little longer. The vowel sound is not changed unless two different vowels are connected.

Ai is pronounced like a long i (b<u>i</u>te).
E is pronounced like a long a (<u>a</u>te).
A is pronounced like "ah" (h<u>a</u>rm).
O is pronounced like a long o (n<u>o</u>).
U is pronounced like oo (b<u>oo</u>t).

"Sain bain oo?" In Mongolian this means "Are you good?" It is how we greet each other. My name is Naarangerel. That means sunlight. You may call me Naraa. I live with my family in the countryside of Mongolia. We are nomadic herdsmen which means we travel around, finding good places to set up our housing with food for the animals we raise. To make it easier to move around, we live in gers, round tents.

This is my favorite camel. I ride him when we move. My sister Jaargal is putting trays of aarul (hard cheese) on the roof of the ger to dry in the sun. I really like aarul, but some visitors think it is bitter. It's made from the milk of our animals and is a favorite snack.

Did you notice the basket by my feet? It is filled with dung, or dried droppings from our animals.

My sister collects the dung every day by flipping it into a basket she carries on her back. We use it for fuel in our stoves.

The stove sits right in the middle of the ger. It keeps us warm and allows us to cook our food. My mother makes bread every day. But first she makes milk tea which has lots of mare's milk, a little black tea and a pinch of salt. Everyone drinks it.

Please come in and join us in the ger. To enter, you should avoid stepping on the threshold and walk to the left. Usually the men sit on one side of the ger and the women on the other.

First you will be served milk tea. We serve and receive everything with the right hand.

Notice that my sister is mixing the airag that hangs in a leather bag by the door. That is mare's milk that we leave to ferment. It is a special drink for holidays and family gatherings.

   While you drink the tea and visit with my family, my mother will prepare one of our favorite dishes—buuzd. They are dumplings made from mutton (sheep's meat). We hope you will eat a lot.

   For our New Year's celebration—Tsegan Sar (or White Month)—we make hundreds of buuzd. For three days, we visit each other, wishing everyone a good new year, catching up on the news, eating buuzd, and giving gifts.

Another favorite holiday is Nadaam, our Independence Day. We celebrate it July 11th to 13th. During Nadaam, people compete in the three "manly" sports—horse racing, wrestling and archery.

This year, my ten-year-old brother, Bold, will ride in the horse race.

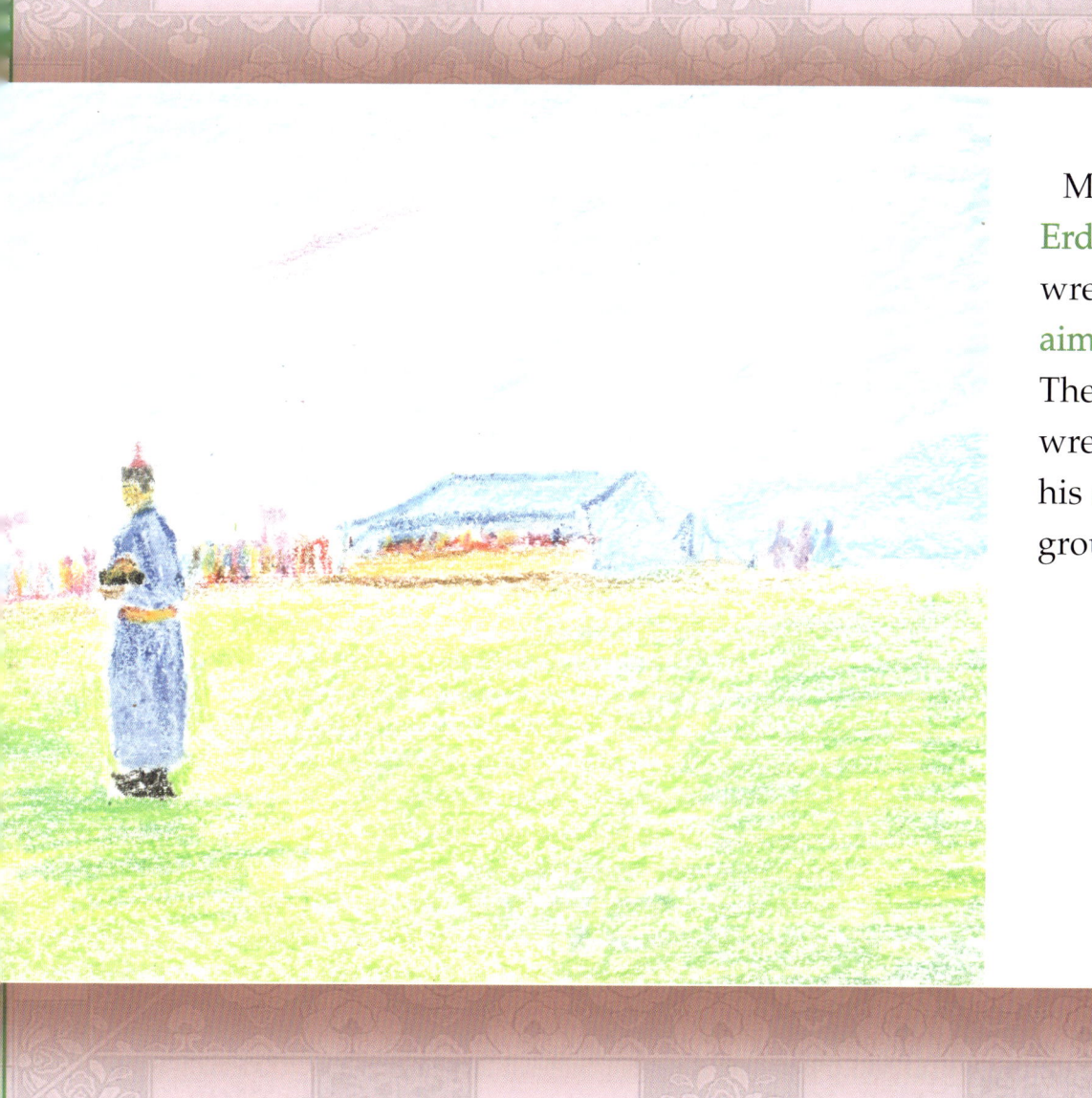

My older brother, Erdene, is the best wrestler in our aimag, or province. The goal of the wrestler is to force his opponent to the ground.

My grandfather will compete in the archery contest. They have to shoot their arrows onto a designated area on the ground.

When Genghis Khan unified Mongolia in the late 12th Century, he led a band of fearsome horsemen and archers into battle. They conquered most of the known world at that time.

Have you noticed that men and women here wear the same clothes? Our outer, long coats are called deels. For everyday use, they are usually rather plain looking, but for holidays, they will be made from bright, silky cloths. We make them ourselves. A bright orange or pink boos (belt) will cinch them at the waist.

It is evening and time to milk the animals again. Come help me with the horses. First, we have the foals drink milk from their mothers; then, we pull them away and gather the mares' milk into a bucket.

Once we finish our chores, we can play with the shagai, or sheep ankle bones. There is a game called shagai, as well as two others called horse races and pick-up-bones. Everyone loves to play games, even our grandparents.

There goes my oldest brother and his family. They are moving their herd to another place. We will join them in another month or so. Notice how easy it is to take down the ger and carry it with them.

I'm glad that you could stay another day. Let's go with my younger brother to take the sheep and goats out to pasture. Depending on what part of Mongolia a herder's family lives in, they might raise goats, sheep, horses, cows, camels, or even yaks.

It can be dangerous being herders because there are sometimes wild animals that stalk the animals in their care. Foxes and wolves especially pose a threat. My brothers, father and grandfather are all very brave men.

In a few years I will have to move into the town and live in a dormitory while I attend school. We go to school through the tenth grade. In fifth grade we begin to learn a foreign language. Russian or English are our choices; I think I'll learn English.

We enjoy visitors anytime, and summer is an especially wonderful time when we have picnics and play games outside. We are so glad you came to share your vacation time with us.

Before you leave, be sure to visit our National Reserve at Terelj. There you will see some of our natural beauty, like the famous "Turtle Rock." Doesn't it look just like a turtle?

You might even see some mountain goats while you are there. But they can be very shy animals, so they may stay out of sight.

I hope you've enjoyed your time in my country. It is a beautiful place to live. Thank you for sharing it with me.

About the Author

Karen Gustafson currently teaches English at North St. Paul High School in Minnesota. She spent three years in Mongolia with ELI (English Language Institute), an organization committed to training Mongolian English teachers. For two of those years she lived and worked in Nalaikh, Mongolia. She hopes that more and more people will come to love the beauty of the Mongolian people and countryside as much as she does.